DK READERS

PROFICIENT
4
READERS

THE PRICE OF
VICTORY

Written by Stewart Ross
Illustrated by Inklink

THE PRICE OF VICTORY

Pylades's story takes place about 2,500 years ago in Ancient Greece. It is the year 416 BCE, and as the athletes prepare for the Olympic Games, the Greek city-states of Sparta and Athens renew their rivalry.

Turn to page 42 to see a map and timeline, and then let the story begin....

"MY NAME IS PYLADES and I am 11 years old. I live with my parents and brother and sister in Athens. My older brother Kinesias is an athlete. He has been training really hard so that he can bring glory to our home city of Athens at the Olympic Games. But we are worried because the gods have sent signs warning Kinesias not to compete in the Games. We do not want to offend the gods but Kinesias is the best runner in all Greece. I must find a way to let him race!"

Words in **bold** appear in the glossary on page 42.

I WENT TO GREET KINESIAS AFTER TRAINING.

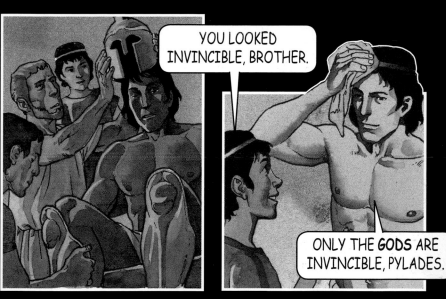

YOU LOOKED INVINCIBLE, BROTHER.

ONLY THE **GODS** ARE INVINCIBLE, PYLADES.

LATER, WE WENT TO UNCLE'S HOUSE FOR A **SYMPOSIUM**.

DON'T BE NERVOUS!

IT WAS ONLY MY SECOND PARTY.

NO ONE WILL BE WATCHING YOU.

DID YOU KNOW? *Guests at symposiums lay on couches.*

LATER, AS WE WERE LEAVING...

...A **SLAVE** GAVE KINESIAS A SLATE.

A STRANGER LEFT YOU THIS!

KINESIAS WENT VERY PALE.

WITHOUT SPEAKING, HE HANDED THE MESSAGE TO ME.

"ATTEND NOT THE GAMES, KINESIAS!"

"I HAVE SPOKEN!"

SIGNED BY ATHENE!

The all-male guests discussed important matters of the day.   11

DID YOU KNOW? *Girls in Athens did not go to school.*

...AN OWL... IN DAYTIME!

THE OWL WAS A SIGN OF ATHENE.

IT WAS A BAD **OMEN**!

I CHASED IT THROUGH THE **AGORA**. SUDDENLY, I HEARD A FAMILIAR VOICE.

PYLADES?

PYLADES! WHERE ARE YOU GOING?

KINESIAS?

AS I TURNED, I SAW SOMETHING FALL FROM A WINDOW ABOVE.

LOOK OUT!

They stayed at home to learn household crafts such as weaving.

DID YOU KNOW? Athene was the patron goddess of Athens.

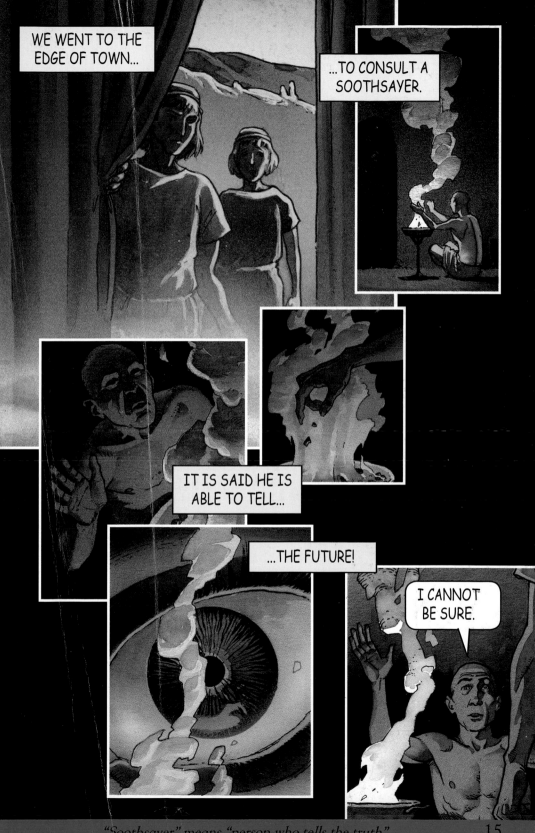

DID YOU KNOW? The most important gods lived on Mount Olympus.

DID YOU KNOW? People came from all over Greece to Delphi.

DID YOU KNOW? Zeus was the most powerful Greek god.

...SEE WHAT YOU CAN FIND OUT.

THIS IS THE PLACE.

COME IN!

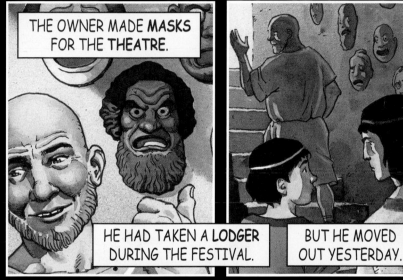

THE OWNER MADE **MASKS** FOR THE **THEATRE**.

HE HAD TAKEN A **LODGER** DURING THE FESTIVAL.

BUT HE MOVED OUT YESTERDAY.

THIS WAS HIS ROOM.

THAT'S ODD!

MY STATUE OF ATHENE IS MISSING!

Festivals were days of feasting dedicated to the gods.

DID YOU KNOW? Only men acted in Greek plays.

AN ACTOR POINTED HIM OUT TO US.

MYRTILOS? YOU'LL FIND HIM UP ON THE...

HEY!

WAIT!

HE SPOTTED US AND TRIED TO GET AWAY.

STOP HIM!

BUT IN SECONDS...

...HE WAS OVER THE OTHER SIDE OF THE STAGE.

DID YOU KNOW? *Dionysos was the god of the theatre.*

I THINK IT'S SPARTAN.

OH...

...HELLO, FATHER...

...MAGISTRATE GOPOLOS...

...COUNCIL MEMBERS!

THE ASSASSIN DROPPED THIS.

ASSASSIN?

DID YOU KNOW? The Greeks were the first to try democracy.

DID YOU KNOW? *Athens had a navy of more than 300 ships.*

DID YOU KNOW? *The Greeks traded goods such as olive oil.*

DID YOU KNOW? *Greek ships carried goods such as wine and grain.*

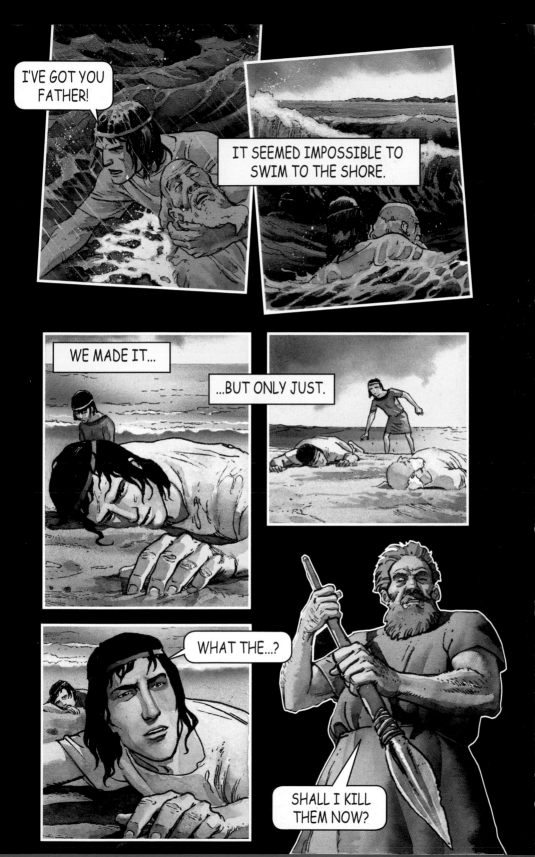

DID YOU KNOW? The helots were the workers in Sparta.

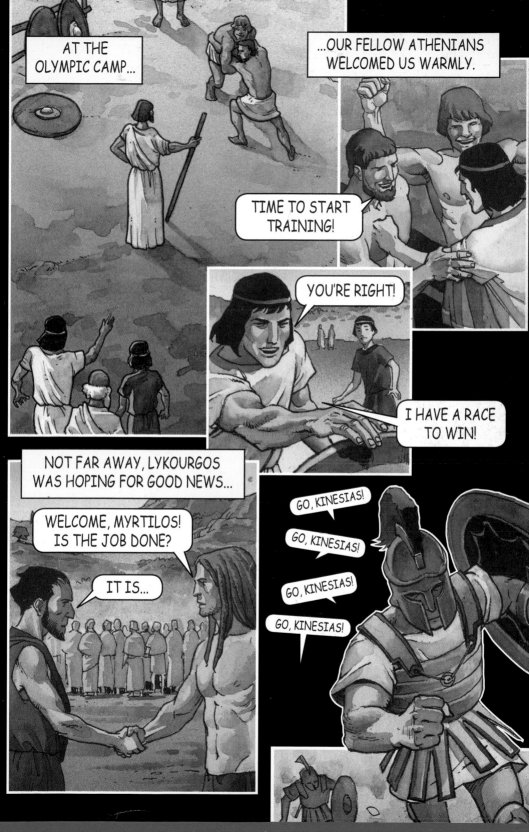

GO, KINESIAS!

GO, KINESIAS!

GO, KINESIAS!

GO, KINESIAS!

IT CAN'T BE!

DON'T WORRY, SIR...

...I - I'M TAKING CARE OF IT.

YOU HAD BETTER BE...

...OR MY FRIEND WILL TAKE CARE OF YOU!

WITH THE FULL MOON, THE GAMES FINALLY ARRIVED.

KINESIAS WAS IN PERFECT HEALTH AGAIN.

WE TOOK PART IN THE OPENING CEREMONY.

DID YOU KNOW?   *The Olympic Games lasted five days.*

DID YOU KNOW? *Greek armour included helmets and shields.*

Twenty-five athletes took part in the race-in-armour.

DID YOU KNOW? About 20,000 spectators watched the Games.

King Menes unites Egypt	Earliest Greek-style civilisation on the island of Crete	First Olympic games are held (according to tradition)
c. 3100	c. 2000	776

3000 BCE (BEFORE COMMON ERA) 2000 BCE 1000 BCE

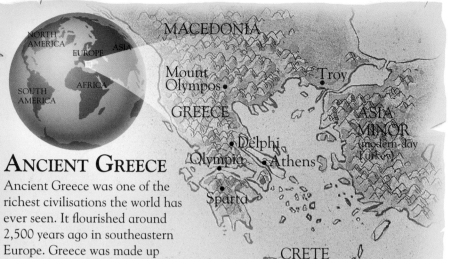

ANCIENT GREECE

Ancient Greece was one of the richest civilisations the world has ever seen. It flourished around 2,500 years ago in southeastern Europe. Greece was made up of several powerful city-states, including Athens and Sparta, that fought each other for control. This beautiful land had a coast on the Mediterranean Sea and included many islands. The sea linked Greece to the known world, spreading its influence across Europe.

GLOSSARY

SPARTA   PAGE 5

The city of Sparta was in the south of Greece. The male Spartans were full-time professional soldiers who were highly trained. Their army was feared across the land.

Soldier / Spartan woman and child   Spartan slave

THE OLYMPIC GAMES   PAGE 5

Athletic games were held all over Greece but the most famous were those held every four years at Olympia – the Olympic Games. There were horse-and-chariot races, as well as many events similar to those at a modern track-and-field competition.

STAGEHAND   PAGE 7

Myrtilos worked at the local theatre helping move scenery around the stage.

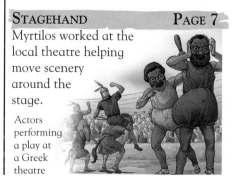

Actors performing a play at a Greek theatre

Romans seize control of mainland Greece	Columbus sails to America	US astronauts land on the Moon

146

1492

1969

TIMELINE

1 CE (COMMON ERA)   1000 CE   2000 CE

YOU ARE HERE

An Athenian family

The Parthenon, a temple dedicated to Athene

Slave

ATHENS   PAGE 7

Athens was the wealthiest and most powerful of the city-states. It was a centre of arts and learning.

Teacher

Pupil

SCHOOL   PAGE 8

Only young male citizens went to school in Athens. They studied reading, writing, music and physical education

GODS   PAGE 9

The Greeks believed in many gods and goddesses, who were immortal (they lived forever). The gods were very powerful and interfered in human lives.

Aphrodite, the goddess of love

Ares, the god of war

Hephaistos, the god of fire and metal-working

Dionysos, the god of parties

43

SYMPOSIUM PAGE 9

The Greeks held private parties called symposiums. These were evenings of drinking and talking held after a meal. Entertainment was provided by musicians and dancers.

ATHENE PAGE 10

Athene was the goddess of war, wisdom and household crafts. She was said to have founded the city of Athens. Her symbol was the owl, which was also the symbol of the city. The Parthenon temple in Athens was dedicated to her.

SLAVE PAGE 11

A slave was someone owned by a Greek citizen. Slaves were usually foreigners captured in war. They did all the hard work for no money.

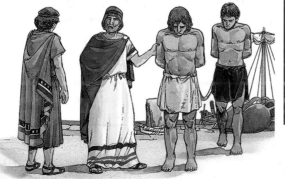

AGORA PAGE 13

Every Greek city had a bustling market square known as the agora. It was full of stalls selling everything from books to pigs and blankets.

SIGN/OMEN PAGES 12 AND 13

The Greeks believed that the gods spoke to them through signs, which could be anything! An omen could be a sign of good or bad luck.

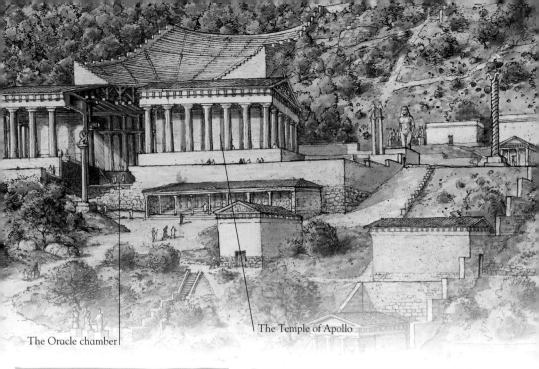

The Oracle chamber

The Temple of Apollo

ORACLE AT DELPHI   PAGE 17

Oracles were places where people could speak to the gods. Delphi, a town on the slopes of Mount Parnassos, was home to the most famous oracle in Ancient Greece. There, a priestess called a Pythia spoke to the gods. She passed the gods' messages on to the people who came to ask for advice.

APOLLO   PAGE 17

Apollo was the god of fortune-telling and truth, as well as music and the sun. The Temple of Apollo at Delphi housed the oracle.

RITUALS   PAGE 18

Rituals are things that have to be done, such as saying particular words, to honour a god.

SACRIFICED   PAGE 18

Animals were sacrificed, or killed, to please the gods. The Ancient Greeks sacrificed valuable animals such as goats or oxen to honour the gods.

An ox being sacrificed

PRIESTESS   PAGE 19

A priestess was a woman who performed ceremonies in honour of the gods.

COMMUNED   PAGE 19

The priestess communed with Apollo, which means she communicated with the god to find out his message.

Zeus and his
wife, Hera

ZEUS   PAGE 20

The Olympic Games took place in
honour of Zeus, who was the king of
the Gods. Zeus threw thunderbolts at
anyone who broke his laws.

THEATRE   PAGE 21

The Ancient Greeks were the first
people to put on plays in special
buildings called theatres. All their
theatres were built outside with
the seats cut in a semicircle into
the hillside and the stage below.

Seats

Stage

MASKS   PAGE 21

Masks were worn by actors on the
stage. Wearing a mask meant that an
actor could play more than one part.
The exaggerated expressions of the
masks made it clear what emotion the
actor was trying to put across.

Masks were made
from a kind of pottery
called terracotta

LODGER   PAGE 21

A lodger is someone who pays to stay
in someone else's house.

AUDIENCE   PAGE 22

The audience is the people who go to watch a play. In the Greek theatre, they sat on stone seats.

SEAL   PAGE 25

Citizens of Greece often carried a seal. This was a metal stamp that was pressed onto a lump of warm wax, lead or clay. The wax was stuck to a letter to show who it was from.

Seal with owner's mark

Wax with the impression left by the seal

COUNCIL   PAGE 26

The Council of Athens was made up of 500 men. They proposed new laws that were discussed at the citizens' Assembly, a meeting of all the male citizens. A group of citizens known as a jury voted on whether or not a man was guilty of a crime.

The Council and Assembly members vote on laws by raising their hands

ASSASSIN   PAGE 26

An assassin is a person hired to kill someone else for money.

DOCKS   PAGE 28

The docks at Peiraieus, 8 kilometres (5 miles) from Athens, were where the Athenian ships came in and out and were loaded and unloaded. Many ships were kept there.

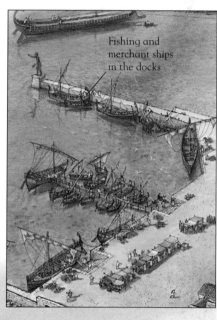

Fishing and merchant ships in the docks

A jury votes by placing tokens into pots

SHIP PAGE 28

Greek merchant ships travelled the Mediterranean Sea trading goods. The ships were made of wood and were pushed along when the wind caught the sails.

Sails were made of cloth

A wooden merchant ship

HELOTS PAGE 34

In Sparta, the helots were the slaves. They were descendants of people conquered by the Spartans. Helots were forced to work as farmers and give half of what they produced to their Spartan masters.

OPENING CEREMONY PAGE 36

A special event to mark the start of the games. The athletes took part and performed special tasks.

The race-in-armour

RACE PAGE 37

The Olympic Games included races, discus, long jump, wrestling and javelin throwing. Kinesias's event, the race-in-armour, was the most exciting and difficult. The athletes raced in full armour, including helmets and shields.